GOOD DOG, CARL

GOOD DOG, CARL

By
Alexandra Day

SCHOLASTIC INC.
New York Toronto London Auckland Sydney

ISBN 0-590-45291-6

12 11 10 9 8 7 6 5 4 3 2   1 2 3 4 5 6/9

Printed in the U.S.A.   23

First Scholastic printing, September 1991

To H.D., who has never let us forget about Ponies

GOOD DOG, CARL

"Look after the baby, Carl.
I'll be back shortly."

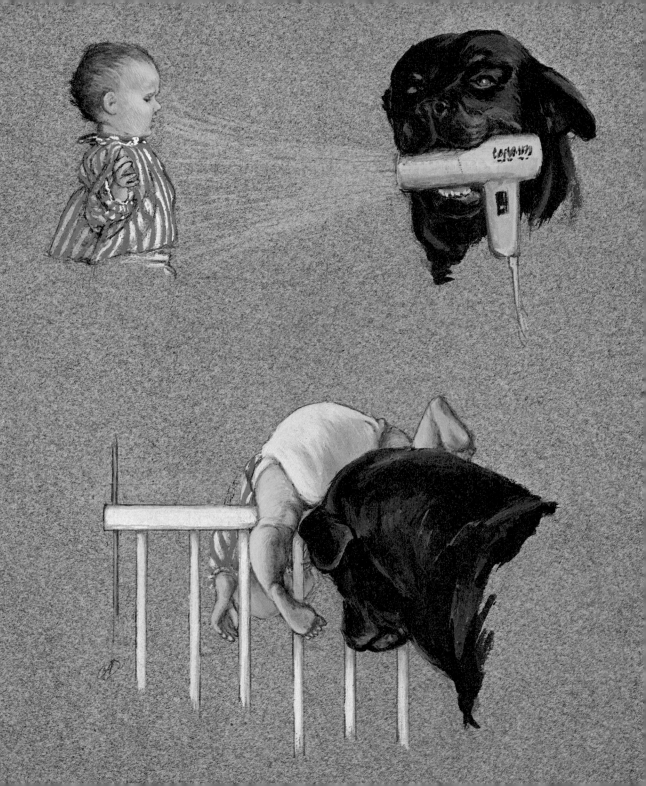

"Good dog, Carl!"

*A salute to the creator of Münchener Bilderbogen No. 1001,
and thanks to Molly Myers and Toby for their sitting talent.*

The paintings for this book were executed in egg tempera.